DATE			

THE SONS OF THE

Dragon Kings

A CHINESE LEGEND

ED YOUNG

ATHENEUM BOOKS *for* YOUNG READERS

NEW YORK LONDON TORONTO SYDNEY

In memory of my sister-in-law, Chien Yuan,
whose interest in the richness of Chinese culture inspired me to introduce its folktales,
and to my nephew, Yang Hong Jian,
who helped with the initial translation

❧

Atheneum Books for Young Readers
An imprint of Simon & Schuster Children's Publishing Division
1230 Avenue of the Americas
New York, New York 10020
Copyright © 2004 by Ed Young

Book design by Michael Nelson
Handlettering by Barbara Bash
The text of this book is set in Hiroshige.
The illustrations are rendered in brush, ink, and cut paper.

Manufactured in China
First Edition
2 4 6 8 10 9 7 5 3 1

LIBRARY OF CONGRESS CATALOGING-IN-PUBLICATION DATA
Young, Ed.
The sons of the Dragon King: a Chinese legend / Ed Young.—1st ed.
p. cm.
Summary: The nine immortal sons of the Dragon King set out
to make something of themselves, and each, with help from a watchful father,
finds a role that suits his individual strengths.
ISBN 0-689-85184-7
[1. Folklore—China.] I. Title.
PZ8.1.Y84Nj 2004
398.2'0951'02—dc21   2002154321

AUTHOR'S NOTE

LONG AGO, Chinese civilization consisted of many tribes. Each tribe believed it was the descendant of a totem animal (similar to that of the northwest Native Americans). There were, for instance, the people of the swallow, and the people of the snake. Over time, however, despite centuries of conflict and strife, these tribes merged together and came to be ruled under one animal—the Dragon King.

The Dragon King is believed to possess a number of features from a variety of animals, including the eyes of the hare, the claws of the eagle, the mane of the lion, the head of the camel, the neck of the snake, the scales of the carp, and the antlers of the deer, combining the many attributes of China's tribes into one triumphant animal.

According to legend, when the Dragon King's nine sons were born, each was as different from the others as the king's features were distinct. And each had a little trouble discovering his own unique talent. It was up to the Dragon King to ensure his royal sons didn't wreak havoc in his kingdom but instead served his people. He clearly did a very good job. . . . The images of his sons can still be found decorating many Chinese objects to this very day.

Different regions of China have different tellings of favorite folktales, and many overlap. The one thing that never varies in the Dragon King folktales is that the king always had nine sons. "The Sons of the Dragon King" is the version I'm most fond of.

BEI-SHE

CHI WEN

PU-LAO

BI-AN

TAO-TIEH

BA-SHA

YA ZI

SUA NI

TIAO TU

IN ANCIENT CHINA

it was said that the Dragon King had nine sons,

each one immortal, each one very different from the next.

As they grew older, each of the sons moved

to a different region of the country to find his place

in the world, far away from the Dragon King's watchful eye.

Alas, it was not long before unsettling rumors

made their way to the king.

The first came from the tutor of his first son, Bei-She. . . .

"Your son does nothing all day, nothing at all, but challenge the peasants in competitions to see if anyone is stronger than he is. This does not seem befitting the son of a king!" the tutor exclaimed.

Indeed it did not. Indeed, such behavior from the son of a king could not be tolerated. Bei-She was meant to discover his talent and make a contribution to his country! So the Dragon King decided to visit his son to set things straight. Disguised as a common peasant, he traveled to the region where Bei-She lived. There he saw Bei-She carrying an enormous weight on his back, racing another man who also carried an enormous weight on his back.

"You see!" cried the tutor. "This is how your son uses his time." The Dragon King was dismayed. He was about to call out to his son and scold him when he suddenly had a thought. Perhaps Bei-She would do well in a position that used his great strength! He beckoned Bei-She to him, and told his son of his idea. Bei-She, pleased that his father had recognized his great strength, readily agreed.

*And to this day,
Bei-She may still be found carrying
the weight of the large columns
that support the roofs of China's
greatest buildings.*

The Dragon King had just returned to his palace when an old servant from the home of his second son, Chi Wen, ran into the throne room.

"A thousand pardons, Your Highness, but I must tell you that your son Chi Wen does nothing all day, nothing at all, but stand upon his roof and stare into the distance. This does not seem befitting the son of a king!" the servant exclaimed.

Indeed it did not. Indeed, such behavior from the son of a king could not be tolerated. The Dragon King slipped his peasant disguise back on and set off for the region where Chi Wen lived. As he approached his son's house, he saw someone standing high on the roof, gazing intently into the distance. It was Chi Wen himself.

The king watched and watched, and his son never moved, except to slowly turn his head back and forth. He seemed to the king to be extraordinarily lazy, and the king was about to shout out to him when he suddenly had a thought. Perhaps Chi Wen was suited for a position that made use of his watchfulness! He called his son down from the roof and told him of his idea. Chi Wen, pleased that his father had recognized his hawklike eyesight, readily agreed.

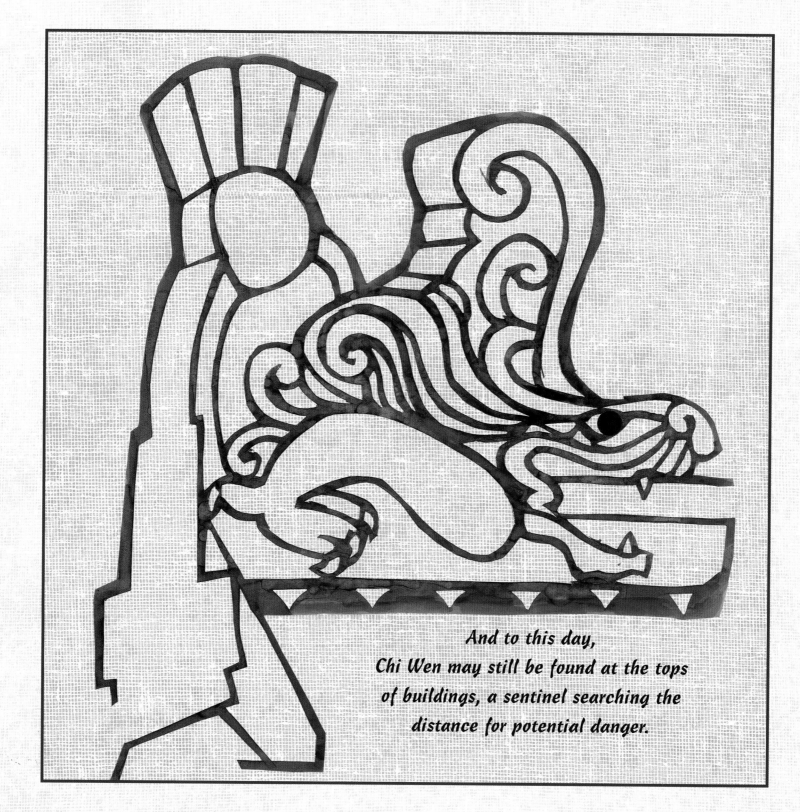

And to this day,
Chi Wen may still be found at the tops
of buildings, a sentinel searching the
distance for potential danger.

Before he could return home, the Dragon King was nearly knocked down by a group of villagers running toward him with their hands covering their ears. They had come from the direction of his son Pu-Lao's house.

"Your son!" they cried. "He does nothing all day, nothing at all, but make the most monstrous noises. This does not seem befitting the son of a king!"

Indeed it did not. Indeed, such behavior from the son of a king could not be tolerated. The king hurried to his son's house, where Pu-Lao bellowed from within. The king thought for a moment. Pu-Lao really didn't have a bad voice; it was just terribly loud. Perhaps he was musical! So the king covered his ears and went into the house to tell his son of his idea. Delighted, Pu-Lao began practicing more earnestly than ever.

And to this day,
Pu-Lao is often seen adorning musical
instruments, no doubt assuring that
their sound will be loud and true.

Pleased, the Dragon King stopped at the home of Bi-An—his fourth son—on his way back to the palace. There he watched from a short distance as Bi-An resolved a dispute between two merchants by carefully weighing their goods on a scale. Wise and eloquent, he settled their disagreement and sent them on their way. Clearly, the king decided, Bi-An must serve the cause of justice. He spoke to his son, who readily agreed, pleased that his father thought him wise.

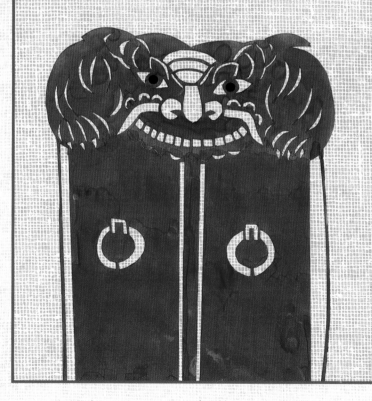

And these many years later,
Bi-An may still be seen supervising
the doorways to the great prisons,
ensuring that only the guilty
are locked inside.

As he returned to his palace, the Dragon King was stopped by the caretaker of his fifth son, Tao-Tieh.

"Ah, good king, I do not like to spread rumors, but your son does nothing all day, nothing at all, but fuss about in the kitchen. This does not seem befitting the son of a king."

The Dragon King frowned deeply, then threw his disguise on once again and rushed toward Tao-Tieh's home, prepared to tell him it wasn't befitting behavior for the son of a king to spend his day in the kitchen. Then he saw a long line of people outside Tao-Tieh's house, standing patiently with bowls in their hands, and he breathed in the most magnificent aroma. He joined the line, and once inside, he saw Tao-Tieh stirring a savory soup for all to share. The people already eating their soup seemed very pleased indeed. The king immediately knew that Tao-Tieh must play a role in the nourishment of the people. Upon hearing his father's idea, Tao-Tieh was so pleased that his father appreciated his cooking that he gave free soup to everyone for the rest of the day.

And today,
Tao-Tieh may still be found protecting
the places where food is prepared
and served.

The Dragon King's sixth son, Ba-Sha, lived fairly close to Tao-Tieh, so the king decided to visit him before returning home. On his way, he heard someone splashing in the Great River. As he drew nearer, he saw that it was his own son frolicking in the water, spraying streams of it from his mouth. The king was shocked. What could he make of such a son? He called to Ba-Sha, who swam so swiftly to him that the king was surprised. He hadn't known his son was such a strong swimmer. That made him think. Perhaps such a good swimmer would do well seeing to the safety of those who used the kingdom's rivers and lakes. Ba-Sha splashed water right onto his father in delight when told of the plan.

And ever since,
Ba-Sha has perched on bridges
crossing the country's waters,
vigilantly watching over those
who pass by in their boats.

When the Dragon King returned home, one of his guards told him
he had heard a rumor: The villagers in his son Ya Zi's province were
afraid of Ya Zi. Although Ya Zi lived in a remote part of the country,
the Dragon King once again donned his disguise and made his way to
his son's home. As he approached, a servant came running from the
house while Ya Zi shouted at him from the door.

"Oh, most revered king!" cried the servant. "The seventh son does
nothing all day, nothing at all, but shout and scream and yell and holler. This does
not seem befitting the son of the Dragon King!" Several villagers nearby nodded.

The king looked at Ya Zi's angry face and wondered what to do
with such a son. He was about to scold him when he realized
that with his temperament, Ya Zi would be well suited for
a position in the military, where he could direct
his anger at the enemy. When he told this
to his son, Ya Zi hollered, "Yes, sir!"
and marched off excitedly.

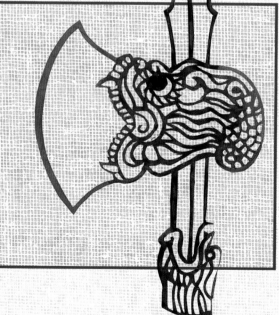

And today,
Ya Zi may still be seen
emblazoned on the weapons
that strike fear
in the country's
enemies.

Unlike Ya Zi, the Dragon King's eighth son, Sua Ni, looked
fearsome but had a kindly heart. So the king was surprised
when a monk from Sua Ni's province caught up with
him on the road to tell him that the eighth son
did nothing all day, nothing at all, but play
with fire. The Dragon King sighed a great
sigh and set off to visit Sua Ni.

When he arrived at Sua Ni's
home, his son was tending to a
flame that he believed would
burn eternally, while patiently
explaining to young children
its importance. The Dragon
King thought hard and
decided that such a kind
heart and such passion
would serve Sua Ni well
in a religious role. Sua
Ni was delighted that
his father approved of
his interest.

Since then,
Sua Ni has been found
embellishing the pots and stands
that hold incense during
religious ceremonies.

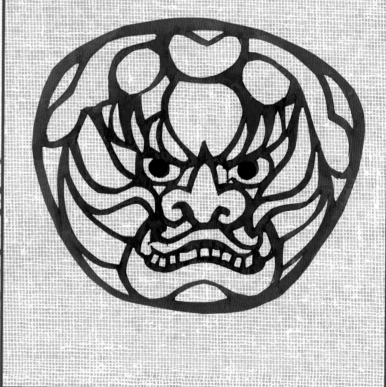

Before anyone else could come up to him with another rumor, the Dragon King took it upon himself to visit Tiao Tu, the ninth son. He found his son's home surrounded by high walls, and when he knocked at the thick, heavy door, no one answered. A little girl passing by shook her head. "Ninth son does nothing all day, nothing at all," she told the king, "unless he can do it from behind the walls of his palace." She bowed low.

Well, such behavior was hardly befitting the son of the Dragon King, the king knew. So he banged and banged and banged again on the door. When the door opened the slightest crack, the Dragon King forced his way through, prepared to scold his son. What could he do with a son with such a disposition? Then he thought, perhaps . . . perhaps in some way Tiao Tu could serve to protect people from unwanted intruders. . . .

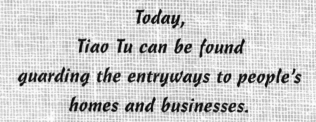

Today,
Tiao Tu can be found
guarding the entryways to people's
homes and businesses.

With great relief, the Dragon King returned home. He took off his disguise and smiled for the first time in a very long time. For now he knew he would hear no more unsettling rumors about his nine sons. And indeed he did not, for each of his sons happily undertook the role he was most suited for—a role befitting the son of the Dragon King—and through the ages, has never ceased to honor his royal heritage and responsibility.

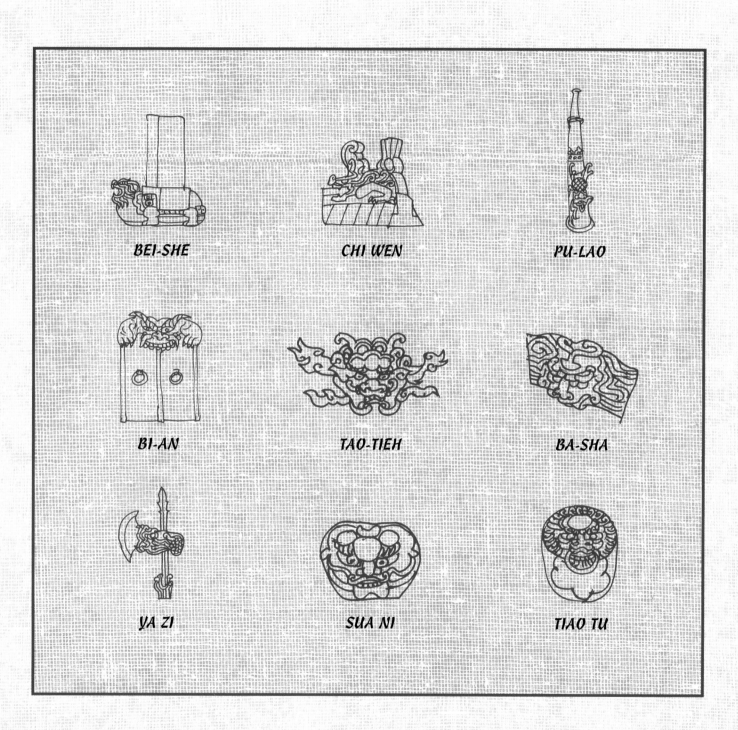

BEI-SHE

CHI WEN

PU-LAO

BI-AN

TAO-TIEH

BA-SHA

YA ZI

SUA NI

TIAO TU